Wilberforce
and the Blue Cave

'*E bella!*' exclaims Nelson the crab when he
beholds the Blue Cave, to which Wilberforce
has taken him and their friend Melody the
shrimp for their holidays. The Blue Cave
is situated in a bay off the coast of Italy,
where they are looked after by Momma, a
kind, motherly cat-fish, and Otto the
octopus. Fun and excitement abound –
Wilberforce has trouble eating spaghetti, a
volcano erupts and the three friends have a
perilous encounter with water spouts, but
all ends splendidly with a historical regatta
where Wilberforce is the star attraction.

Leslie Coleman, author of this book and
its predecessor *Wilberforce the Whale*, also
in Beavers, originally created the characters
for a radio programme, and the stories are
particularly good for reading aloud.

Wilberforce and the Blue Cave

Leslie Coleman

Illustrations by John Laing

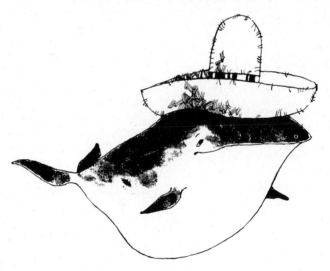

Beaver Books

First published in 1974 by
Blackie and Son Limited
Bishopbriggs, Glasgow G64 2NZ

This paperback edition published in 1977 by
The Hamlyn Publishing Group Limited
London · New York · Sydney · Toronto
Astronaut House, Feltham, Middlesex, England

© Copyright Text Leslie Coleman 1974
© Copyright Illustrations on pages 18, 40, 51, 52,
62, 85
The Hamlyn Publishing Group Limited 1977
© Copyright remaining illustrations
Blackie and Son Limited 1974
ISBN 0 600 39386 0

Printed in England by
Hazell Watson and Viney Limited
Aylesbury, Bucks
Set in Imprint

Contents

I

The Unexpected Holiday

Melody, the shrimp, was playing jacks with her small crab friend, Nelson, in the sandy space outside her cave. It was Nelson's turn to throw, and he was just scuttling round picking up the five small chips of stone, when there was a cheerful, rumbling shout beyond the braided-leaf weed that sloped downhill from the cave into deeper water.

'Tally-ho, my little shore shavers, my finny little friends! Are you there?'

'It's him,' said Nelson, dropping the stone chips and setting off with his funny sideways scuttle as fast as he could.

'We're here, Wilberforce,' cried Melody, swimming ahead—pfut-pfut-pfut.

'Ah, my cheeky little sea-urchins, there you are!' boomed the whale, as all sixty feet of his great body thrust excitedly into the cove.

'There's news! Oh, there's news indeed! Just you listen while I tell you, you lucky little people!' And he burst into a rumbling song:

'If you go down to the woods today,
You're in for a big surprise . . .'

'A surprise! A surprise!' cried Nelson. 'Oh, go on; *do* tell!'

But Wilberforce had done a sudden, excited turn—per-rump-ah!—and dashed across the cave to where a fat Pout fish was puffing round a weed-covered rock. The Pout was loaded with a lot of square black boxes of various sizes, which hung about his body on leather straps.

'Ah, Mr Pout,' beamed Wilberforce, 'good of you to come! Do you think you can take them here?'

'Certainly, Mr Whale, certainly!' puffed the fat Pout, setting down his load of black boxes. 'Anywhere will do, anywhere at all!' And he started to put things out and screw things up with remarkable speed and dexterity for one so fat and breathless. 'This will do very nicely indeed.' And he screwed two bits together and pulled out three collapsible legs. 'In fact just the place for an artistic photographic study!'

Almost like a conjuring trick, he assembled a camera on its tripod with a piece of black velvet over it, and two floodlights on either side pointed at a flat rock in the middle of the cove which was bathed in bright light.

'Oh,' said Nelson dejectedly, 'I had my photo taken at school, and the photographer said, "watch for the little flying-fish!" but it never came. I think photos are dull. Do we *have* to have our photos taken, Wilberforce?'

'Of course we do,' said Wilberforce, turning round and grinning all over. 'That's the great news—our summer holiday. We're going abroad, so we shall need passport photos.'

'Where's abroad?' asked Nelson.

'Away from home waters in another sea,' said Wilberforce, 'where it's all blue and sunny. And you have a sort of a book, which is called a passport, and you stick your photo in it. Then, when you come to the border, you show this passport to the Customs Officer, and he looks at you, and he looks at the photo, and he says, "Yes, that's you, you can come in".'

'But I know it's me without looking at my photo,' said Nelson, puzzled.

'Well, that's what they do,' said Wilberforce.

'Photos! Oh, why didn't you tell me before?'

cried Melody, flustered. 'I haven't done my feelers. I know I look an absolute fright!'

'Just put on your coral clasp, and you'll look splendid,' said Wilberforce kindly.

'Oh, do you think so?'

'I'm sure of it.'

So Melody disappeared—pfut-pfut!—into her cave.

'Perhaps,' suggested Mr Pout, 'perhaps Mr Whale would care to sit while Madam is getting herself ready. Just head and shoulders, I think.'

'Well, the head by all means,' grinned the whale, taking his place on the brightly-lit rock, 'but as for the shoulders, you'll have some difficulty in finding *them*. The tail, yes! The tum, yes! But as for . . .'

'Quite so,' wheezed Mr Pout, and they both laughed.

Then the photographer started disappearing in and out of the piece of black velvet behind the camera, and twiddling the lens in front, and bringing this light nearer, and that light further, and for some moments he was very busy indeed.

After a bit, Nelson could contain himself no longer, and asked

'How did you decide we were going abroad?'

'Ah, my little rambling rover,' grinned Wilberforce, 'thereby hangs a tale:'

> 'A whale of a tale,
>   Or the tail of a whale?
>   Please tell us quickly;
>   You're slow as a snail!'

chanted Melody from her cave, where she had been listening all the while.

'OK, then,' replied her big friend, 'You remember my Aunty Barnacle?'

'Your rich, adopted Aunty Barnacle, who lives in a Scottish loch?'

'That's the one,' said Wilberforce. 'Well, she had mermeasles very badly—oh, excr-r-r-ruciating itchiness! So when she was better, the sturgeon said she needed a thorough holiday in a warm and sunny climate, and so she rented this little place in the Mediterranean Sea,'

'If you could sit quite still for a moment, please,' interrupted the photographer.

Wilberforce went absolutely rigid with a smile rather like a shark saying how-do-you-do to its dinner. 'This photographic modelling business—very skilled!' he muttered out of the corner of his mouth.

'A little relaxed! ... Splendid!' said Mr Pout, and then quite suddenly a little black thing he was holding up in his right fin went 'puff-click!' and there was a blinding flash. Melody said 'Oh!' Everybody jumped, and Wilberforce nudged one of the lamps over on its side so that it pointed at the top of the sea.

'I'm very sorry,' said the whale.

'Not to worry,' wheezed Mr Pout. 'Should have warned you I was using flashlight.'

And while he was putting things to rights, Wilberforce went on about his Aunty Arabella Barnacle's 'little place' in the Mediterranean.

'It's a beautiful cave in a beautiful island and it's called the "Blue Cave",' he continued enthusiastically, 'and it's the loveliest cave in the world. Well, now my aunty is better and able to come home, there's no one there to enjoy it, so she wants us all to go out and stay. And she says she wants the journey to be as enjoyable as the rest of the holiday, so she has got her travel agents to arrange the whole thing for us, and they're going to drop their plans in today.'

'Well, let's try again,' said Mr Pout cheerfully and this time everything went splendidly— puff-flash-click! 'And now the young lady!' he wheezed.

'Yes,' said Wilberforce flopping off the rock, 'they're dropping the plans in today; a chart of the best route, I expect: and we shall start as soon as possible.'

'Goody, goody!' cried Nelson, as Melody came out of her cave, and she really did look very pretty with her feelers all combed in her pink coral clasp.

'Charming! Delightful!' said Mr Pout—puff-flash-click!—and the snap was taken almost before Melody had settled on the rock.

'Already!' said Melody, quite disappointed.

Then it was Nelson's turn, and he was just scrambling onto the rock when there was a sound in the distance—per-lomp-er-lomp-er-lomp-er-lomp-er-lomp.

'Boat ho, my midget messmates!' warned Wilberforce, and everybody lay quite still as the boat drew nearer and slowed down. As it passed overhead there was a 'splash', and something was thrown into the sea. Then the boat accelerated — per-lomp-er-lomp-er-lomp-er-lomp-er-lomp—and made off again.

Everybody looked upwards. Floating down towards them was a very large, bulky and important-looking envelope tied with blue string and sealed with red sealing-wax.

'It's the plans for our holiday. They've dropped them in as they promised!' cried Melody.

The important-looking envelope sank slowly down, wobbling from side to side as flat objects do in water, and everybody wanted to be the one to catch it. So Wilberforce swam a little to the right . . . and Melody swam a little to the right . . . and Nelson scuttled a little to the right on his rock. Then Nelson moved a little to the left . . . and Melody moved a little to the left . . . and Wilberforce moved a little to the left, and all heads strained upwards, not looking at anything but the envelope.

At this point Mr Pout remembered what Wilberforce had just done to his lamps and became acutely anxious about them, and *he* started swimming backwards and forwards, a little to the left and a little to the right. And the envelope wobbled slowly downwards. The three friends looked at the envelope, and Mr Pout looked at the lights, but nobody looked at Mr Pout's own tail, which just then got caught in one of the light's wires, and this in turn got caught round the camera stand.

'Oh, the camera! Save my camera! Oh goodness, my gracious, oh me!' gasped Mr

Pout, as all his precious equipment started to topple over.

Of course, everyone came to the rescue at once. The sea got all stirred up, and instead of falling over, the camera started to bob upwards, and so everybody bobbed up with it rather like a slowed-down picture of the Harlem Globe Trotters playing basketball.

At last Melody got hold of one leg of the tripod, and Mr Pout got hold of Melody, and Wilberforce got hold of them both, and they managed to get the camera up again on the sea-bed.

'Well, now for the young gentleman,' said Mr Pout, but instead of Nelson on the rock between the two lumps there lay the important-looking envelope all bound up with blue string and red sealing-wax.

'Nelson!' they called, but there was no answer. On the other hand the important-looking letter was getting very talkative indeed.

'Lemme-out! Where-am-I? Gemme-outer-here!' it shouted in angry if slightly muffled tones, and it started to give indignant little bounces.

'Oh dear,' laughed Wilberforce, and swimming to the rock he picked the envelope up.

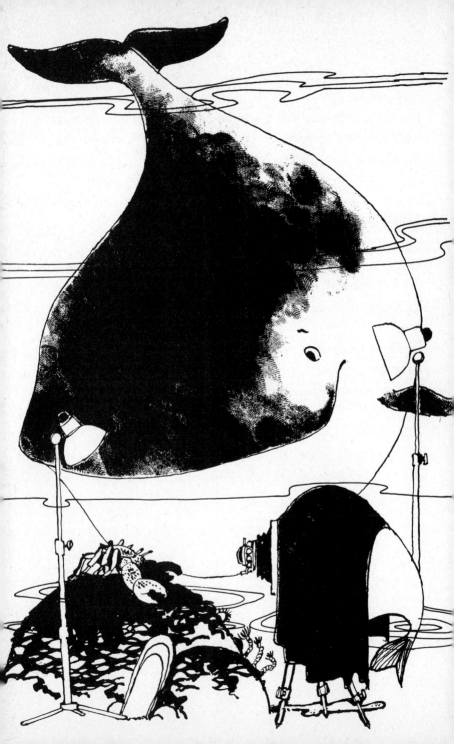

There underneath, rather squashed and very red, was poor Nelson who had been the one to catch the plans but had found their weight too much for him.

'I was very nearly totally and completely spiflicated,' the poor little crab spluttered, and it looked as if he was going to burst into tears at any moment. But when Wilberforce promised that *he* should be the one to break the red sealing-wax on the important-looking envelope, he brightened up at once.

Almost before Nelson realised what had happened, Mr Pout had gone—puff-flash-click!

'Thank you very much! I'll be right back with the prints,' he said. His apparatus melted back into the black boxes, and the tubby Mr Pout, still puffing and panting, and looking like a Christmas-tree with all his belongings strung around him, disappeared. The three friends were left with the important-looking envelope, tied up with blue string and red sealing-wax, on the rock in the middle of the cove.

2

All Aboard

Nelson didn't wait to be told twice to undo the important-looking envelope, and with the others lending an excited fin a rainbow-coloured pile of papers soon poured out onto the rock, like the contents of a giant Christmas cracker.

'This must be where we're going,' cried Melody, spreading out a large map on the sea-bed.

'And this,' put in Wilberforce, concentrating fiercely on another coloured sheet, 'this says it's our ret-er-in . . . our er . . . rin-y-tin . . . er . . . our ar-y-int . . . our . . .'

'Our it-in-er-ary,' Melody spelled out. 'That's how we get there.'

'But of course,' agreed Wilberforce, 'that's just what I was saying—our "how-we-get-there" . . . and floundering fluke-fins! We start today!'

'And this says, "Return tickets for the boat",' cried Nelson.

'Boat!' exclaimed Wilberforce.

'Fish on a boat!' cried Melody.

'Of course it would save time.'

'But even if we *did* get on board . . .'

'How could we swim about?'

'Or . . . anything?' concluded Nelson.

There was a long questioning pause.

'You don't think your Aunty Barnacle has made a mistake?' said Nelson doubtfully.

'My Aunty Barnacle *never* makes a mistake,' replied Wilberforce. 'If she says we're going by boat, we shall *go* by boat. I don't know how, but . . .'

At that instant a deep sound reverberated through the waters of the cove—Hoo-oo-oo!

Pish-per-soof!—Everyone spun round. Out at sea a huge black shadow was looming into view. It was so long and so vast that it seemed as though it would go on for ever.

'Is it a floating island, do you think?' asked Nelson, worried.

'It's a ship, silly,' explained Melody.

'But it's gi-normous!' cried Nelson.

'It's an ocean-going cargo ship,' said Wilberforce, 'and I shouldn't wonder, my microscopic little merchant mariners, if it wasn't *our* ship.'

But Melody's attention had been drawn elsewhere. 'Look! Look over there!' she interrupted suddenly.

Her two friends turned in the direction she was pointing. Swimming towards them was a shoal of the oddest-looking fish. They were all black in colour. Goggly eyes protruded from a round blob at the front of each oblong body, which had four tendril-sort of things attached at the four corners, and they all had humps on their backs.

The three friends froze absolutely still.

'It's . . . it's . . .!' gasped Melody.

'It's skin-divers,' said Nelson. 'I don't like skin-divers; they have harpoon-guns and things sometimes.'

'Wait!' said Wilberforce in his 'emergency' voice.

Just where the sandy sea-bed started to shelve downwards from the shallower waters, the strangers halted. Then one of them swam quietly forward over the bladderwrack. He didn't seem to be paying them any particular attention at all, and Melody and Nelson started to feel a little easier.

When he was still several paces away, the diver took something out of a pouch which was slung over his shoulder and put it on a rock. Then he backed off. Presently the tide started to wash tiny crumbs from the mysterious object. Wilberforce's nose twitched.

'Cuttlefish!' he murmured, and—peroosh!— he eased forward ever so slightly. 'Mm-m-m, the best cuttlefish!' His nose twitched again, and—peroosh!—he eased forward a little further. 'The sort of cuttlefish my Aunty Barnacle keeps for special treats. . . . I think I'd better investigate.' And—per-rump-ah!—the great whale was gone.

'Oh, Wilberforce, is it safe?' cried Melody.

But already her big friend had not only gulped the cuttlefish off the rock, but was taking a second helping which the skin-diver held out to him. And then all of a sudden they started to play, and it would have made a catfish laugh to see them loop and roll and chase round in circles, and there could be no possible doubt that *this* diver was friendly. Then three more came up and beckoned Wilberforce out towards the great ship. As he went the whale gave Melody and Nelson a grin and flipped his fluke tail to them as if to say, 'It's all OK.'

'I think this must be part of Aunty Barnacle's plan,' said Melody. So when another skin-diver appeared and beckoned them too, Melody and Nelson swam over and said, 'How-do-you-do,' and the man smiled back through his goggles, and in no time at all they had swum into a large and luxurious aquarium tank, which was being carried up the ship's companion-way. As they went, Nelson counted the rows of portholes.

'. . . three . . . four . . . FIVE!' he exclaimed excitedly, 'It's a *liner* that we're on!'

Then the tank was gently put down, and they started to explore their new quarters. It was a comfortable tank with sand at the bottom and green string weed and piles of rocks and stones, and Nelson found that if you scrambled far enough up one of the piles, you came right out on top and could look round the whole ship.

'What's going on up there?' Melody called.

'Well, we're at the front end, and there's the bridge and three more decks above us. It's absolutely fantastic,' Nelson exclaimed bubbling over. 'And there's a . . . one of those crane things leaning out from the mast.'

'A derrick,' suggested Melody.

'Yes, and there's a rope running down from it over the side from an engine on deck. And they're hauling something up,' Nelson went on, and Melody could hear the 'whee-ee-ee-ee-ee-ee' of a modern electric motor.

'What are they bringing aboard?' she asked.

'I can't see yet,' replied Nelson, 'but it's heavy . . . very heavy. . . . Yes, here it comes! I can just see the top. . . . It's something very big. It's Wilberforce!'

And there, over the side, padded with seaweed and held by four strong hawsers, Wilberforce rose with a glorious grin all over his good-natured face.

'First floor, gents' ready-to-wear, boots and shoes and ironmongery,' he called as up he went like a lift. 'Roof garden! Mind the step, please!' he beamed as the derrick came to a halt. Then the arm began to swing inboard. 'Ahoy there, my crabby little cruise-mate!' he called, spotting Nelson. 'As good as a fun fair. What a ride!'

At this point the derrick started to let him down towards a large tank on the deck below.

'Oh he flies through the air
With the greatest of ease,
That daring young whale
On the flying trapeze.
Tiddly-ompty-pom-pom . . . Oh!'

And just as Wilberforce was reaching the end of the chorus, the hawser, which was steadily unwinding, came to a sudden halt.

'Per-umpty-pom . . . Oh!' continued the whale as the hawser suddenly slipped another three feet and jerked to a stop again.

Down below the motorman was doing something complicated with a spanner, and an officer had come forward and was staring at the works in a questioning way. It looked as if there was a bit of a breakdown. Up above, Wilberforce swung gently to and fro in mid-air.

'Hey, Wilberforce!' shouted Nelson presently, waving one of his little claws, 'what are you doing up there?'

'I am rehearsing my part for our Christmas pantomime,' replied the whale with pretended dignity.

'What's that?' asked Nelson.

'The Fairy Queen,' grinned Wilberforce.

Melody put her head out of water and began one of her chants:

'Though he floats in the blue in a manner so airy,
 Our Wilberforce seems rather fat for a fairy.
 Of course, you might think he's the man in the moon,
 But to me he looks more like a barrage balloon!'

'You rude thing!' laughed Wilberforce.

'Never mind,' sympathised Melody. 'I expect they'll get you down soon. Have you got a nice view?'

'Positively panoramic, my shrimpy little shipmite! I can see for miles and miles and miles. It's like being a seagull,' he called back. 'But it's warm, distinctly warm!' And poor Wilberforce began to puff and pant because, as everyone knows, although a whale is a mammal and breathes air, if he is long out of water he dries up and suffers terribly from the heat.

'Ship ahoy!' he gasped, 'I'm boiling.'

Fortunately the officer understood about animals, and already orders had been given. Deckhands came running, a long snaky length of fire-hose was unreeled along the deck, and a pump was coupled up. Then somebody gave the order, 'Water on!' and a jet from the nozzle rose to play on Wilberforce's back.

'Oh delightful! Oh glorious! Oh exquisite!' cried the whale. 'Just a little nearer the shoulder-blade, please! . . . Oh bliss!' he added as the cooling water crept comfortingly over his body.

Just then, an urgent voice sounded from down below in the sea.

'Hey!' it said, and then there was a 'plosh!' as a fat body fell back into the water. 'Hey!' it came a second time, 'you've forgotten . . . "plosh!" . . . your passport . . . "plosh!" . . . photographs . . . "plosh!"'

Wilberforce looked down to see Mr Pout, good as his word, leaping out of the water like a flying-fish in an effort to deliver the precious pictures. But what could the whale do, held up as he was in mid-air? What if they couldn't even start their holiday because their passports weren't complete!

Fortunately the last of the skin-divers was just climbing onto the bottom landing of the companionway, and he saw Mr Pout leaping out of the water at its foot. Immediately he grasped the precious package, which contained not only the photographs but their tickets and passports as well!

'Good-bye!' gasped the kindly Pout as he whizzed through the air for the last time. 'Enjoy yourselves!' and he fell back into the water with a final 'plosh!'

'Thank you,' called the whale, and then— whee-ee-ee-ee-ee—came the welcome sound of the motor, and the hawser started to lower Wilberforce into his special tank below. There he was snugly fitted in and packed all round with seaweed which was kept damp with jets of running water. Then a donkey-engine started up, drawing in the massive anchor chain— checker-up, checker-up, checker-up—and the chain was still crawling steadily in as 'ching-ching-ching!' went the bridge telegraph to the engines below, and the decks began to pulse with power. The ship's siren gave a long blast— Hoo-oo-oo-oo-oo-oo!

The voyage had begun.

3

The Eight-fisted Fight

And it was a most enjoyable voyage. Nelson spent most of the time at the top of the rocks in his aquarium keeping a sharp look-out through a piece of drinking straw, which he used as a telescope; and there always seemed to be at least three or four ships in sight to report to Melody below. Wilberforce fell into a holiday mood straight away and used one of Aunty Barnacle's Celtic runes to make himself a white pork-pie hat like they have in the American navy, and he pushed this jauntily over one eye, which made all the deck-hands laugh. And their own special steward brought them meals, 'At more than frequent intervals,' as Melody put it, and Wilberforce described their routine of eating and sleeping and watching other ships go by as:

' "A.1. at Lloyd's," my little touring tittle-bats!'

The weather changed from grey rolling clouds with sudden cold showers of rain, to pale blue vistas drifting with whispy white, and at last to deep blue skies with only occasional puffs of cottonwool, and it started to get so hot that the three friends took to having a siesta after meals.

It was during one of these naps some days later that all three of them awoke together. There was something strange in the air.

'What's wrong?' asked Nelson.

'The engines!' cried Melody. 'They've stopped!'

Then there was a loud 'splosh!' and a rattle of chains as the anchor was cast.

'We're there!' cried Wilberforce.

'Hooray!' shouted Nelson.

And they looked out to find themselves anchored in the middle of a most beautiful blue bay—blue sky, blue water and, at this distance, even blue land with a back-drop of blue mountains white snow-flecked at the top, piercing a shimmering haze.

Soon the ship became very busy indeed. Deck-hands were everywhere. The companionway was let down. 'Ching-ching-ching,' went the bridge telegraph—'finished with engines!' The derrick was swung out. A little motorboat came alongside, and strange officials with sun-tanned faces and grey uniforms swarmed aboard, and everybody seemed to be talking more with their hands than their faces.

Then an officer with a rather fierce moustache came and picked up their passports. For a moment the moustache bristled with concentration, and Melody thought that something awful must be wrong. Then the dark face cleared, and gave a great smile filled with white teeth.

A moment later Wilberforce was hoisted out of his tank and dropped over the side, while Melody and Nelson were carried down the companionway and gently released into the sea.

'Good-bye!' they called, and started to dive—blabble-abble-ebble-ibble . . . But before they were half-way down—sfish-sfash-sfish, sfish-sfash-sfish—they were mobbed by hoards of darting sea creatures of all shapes and colours and sizes.

'Taxi!' cried a big, fat, booming sun fish on one side, and on the other,

'Chocolate-a, meester, you give?' begged a

chubby, cheeky little anchovy. Then a rainbow wrasse in a peaked uniform cap bustled up;

'Very good-a guide! Take-a you all over?'

And more and more fish swarmed around, some pulling this way, some pushing that and all jabbering and arguing amongst themselves till Nelson cried out in astonishment;

'They don't talk like us; I don't understand what they are saying.'

'We're abroad now,' said Melody. 'They always speak differently abroad.'

'Oh!' said Nelson. 'How do we tell them what we want, then?'

'You speak very slowly,' said Wilberforce, 'and loudly; then they'll understand,' and he began to force his way through the crush to the sea bed, taking his own advice and repeating very slowly and loudly,

'NO . . . THANK . . . YOU! EXCUSE . . . ME . . . PLEASE!' and at last he managed to open out the map to see where to go, but even then everyone crowded round to look over his shoulder.

'Where the signor wish-a to be?' enquired an ingratiating voice behind them.

'We are trying to find the Blue Cave,' said Wilberforce speaking slowly and loudly.

'Ah-ha, ze Blue-a Cave—*bella*, *bella*! Is beautiful!' the voice continued. 'You come with me!'

The babble of tongues was hushed. There was a whispered exclamation—'Gaspare!' Small fry at the back inched nervously away. The three friends turned round to find themselves facing—a shark! Not a particularly big shark, but a shark with a moth-eaten and unkempt air about him, with piggy little eyes too close together, and a nasty gash in one flank from a fight no doubt; and he was wearing a smile . . . a smile like a sharp steel trap!

'The Blue Cave? I take-a you *dirretto*, straight, no?' And then he saw Melody. '*Ah-ha, che regazza simpatica*, is pretty, no!' and he eased forward with an even nastier grin. You could see his sharp yellow-brown teeth, some broken, some missing, some decayed.

Melody shrank back towards her big friend. 'I don't like him,' she whispered. 'Please, we don't want *him* for a guide.'

And Nelson added 'Definitely not!'

'The Blue Cave, ha? I show!' and the shark turned as if to lead the way. But a chubby small fry on the inner edge of the crowd had swum a little too close and momentarily blocked his path. With a scythe-like movement, the shark's tail caught the little fellow a vicious cuff that sent him sprawling, and he started to whimper. The shark gave an ugly snarl. Then the oily smile returned.

'Ah, the beautiful Blue Cave—*bellissima, bellissima*! I go! You come!'

'We're not going to let a bully like that take us,' whispered Melody.

For once, Wilberforce was nonplussed. He would have liked to give the wretched brute a lesson, but here he was, a visitor in strange waters, and it would be poor manners to his hosts to start a rumpus within five minutes of arriving.

'I think it would be too expensive to have a guide. We can find our own way, thank you,' he said coldly.

'Who speak-a of money? First I get you there—then we talk,' and the piggy little eyes squinted at them craftily.

'*Scusa*! If you please!' cut in a cheery voice behind them, and — schiff-fussz! — into the space between them shot a small reddish-brown 'comet'. Schiff-up!—the comet came to an instant halt and opened out eight tentacles to reveal a humorous, round-faced octopus.

'*Permesso!*' he said. Then bowing politely to Melody, 'the *signorina* will allow?' And without waiting for a reply, he turned swiftly to face the shark.

'*Via, brutto pesce cane! Via, via! Andate subito, sporco pirata!*' And although they couldn't understand a word, the three friends had no doubt that the brave little fellow was telling the shark to go about his business.

The shark's piggy little eyes went red with rage. Sfish!—the head turned and 'snap' went the jaws, but the little octopus just darted comet-like backwards out of reach.

Now if you are going to have to fight (as the shark was!) it is bad enough having to keep a wary eye out for the other chap's left hook, let alone also watching for a possible right jab, but if you are half-blinded with rage, and your opponent has *two* left hooks and *two* right jabs, not to mention another two for personal defence, and even a spare pair to do anything he likes with, you haven't, as the shark soon found, much of a chance.

'Poom!' went a crisp right, slap where the shark's left ear might be supposed to be. Then, 'piff-paff-boink!' went arms number two, three and four on his nose. Then—sfish—the little

comet streaked right under the brute and 'bink-boink-bink-boink!' entirely regardless of the Queensberry Rules, there was a sharp tattoo of kicks with legs five, six, seven and eight just where the shark might be supposed to sit down —if sharks do sit down—and this was followed by 'biff-baff-bam!' a brisk rat-a-tat on his left eye. And all the while there was an ear-splitting volley of:

'*Via! Via, ladro!*'

And no matter how the shark turned and snapped or swished his tail, the little octopus was always darting out of range, and although the blows weren't very heavy, the shark was being made to look so stupid that the crowd began to titter, and presently the brute turned tail and slunk away, muttering darkly.

'That was quite splendid,' said Wilberforce admiringly as the crowd started to melt away.

'*Prego!* Not to mention,' and the octopus waved a nonchalant arm. 'By all he is known here, Gaspare, the pirate! It is nothing. I, Otto, can fight like-a him . . . how you say? with seven-a hands tied behind me!' And he struck a dramatic pose with chest stuck out and little fists up, till Melody wanted to laugh, he looked so quaint.

'Permit, please, the pleasure to present myself,' he continued, 'Ottoditi, Cesare Fabiano Garibaldi Vincenzo Mario Bartholomeo!'

And he threw out two arms to shake Wilberforce by the fin.

'I have looked long time for-a to see you, Ou-ilberforz-a, and you too, little Melody shreemp,' and he bowed very gallantly over her right pincer. ('Quite romantical!' as she told her friend, Stella, later back home.) 'And *eccola*! The leetle-a crab, Nelson *è justo*, is right, ha?' and he patted the little fellow warmly on the shell with yet another arm.

'We're very glad to meet you Mr er . . . Mr er . . .' began Wilberforce.

'Otto! You call-a me Otto, same like my other friends, ha? Otto, the octopus,' and he continued shaking hands, pumping all three of them up and down at once till Nelson started to feel a bit like a pneumatic drill.

'But Otto, how do you know our names?' asked Melody at last.

'I come-a from the Aunty Arabella—your Aunty Barnacle.'

'My *adopted* Aunty Barnacle,' exclaimed Wilberforce.

'*My* adopted Aunty Barnacle also. So we

adopted cousins—already old-a friends! Is-a good?'

'Is-a *very* good,' laughed Wilberforce, and the others joined in.

'So I come to greet-a you,' Otto went on. 'When my Aunty Barnacle she go to her home-a, she say, "Otto," she say to me, "you must meet them and make them the holiday the best. Give them my love-a and see them the most happy at the Blue Cave." So me, Otto,' and he thumped his chest with an important little fist, 'me, Otto, your guide. You like-a?'

'Indeed, we like,' said the three friends together.

'Then, *andiamo*,' laughed Otto.

'Let's go!' chimed Nelson.

'Already you begin to understand our-a language,' cried Otto.

And taking his lead, they all started off at an easy swim through water so sunny and translucent you could see for miles. In a very short while they rounded the point of a small island.

Otto stopped and threw out all his arms together.

'*Eccola*! Is there!' he exclaimed.

4

At the Blue Cave

'*Eccola*! Is-s there,' cried Otto, as they swam round the base of a sharp basalt rock which jutted steeple-like out of the sea towards the clear blue sky. They were in a small bay, its silver-grey sandy floor dotted with pumice rocks, and in the sheer cliff face in front of them was—the cave! But before they had time to take it all in, Otto cried out,

'*Ecco!* Is-a Momma!' and darted—schiff-fusz, schiff-up—towards a stout little cat-fish who was bustling forward to meet them. She had a red scarf on her head, and wore a small white apron.

'Is-a Momma who keep-a the house,' explained the octopus, throwing four of his eight arms round her with good-natured affection. 'Momma look after *me*! Momma look after *you*! Momma look after *every*bodies!'

And the motherly old cat-fish waddled forward laughing and chattering with him. First there was a welcoming kiss for Melody, next a big hug for Nelson and last she turned to Wilberforce. For a moment her mouth fell open as her eyes, wide with wonder, followed the whale's huge bulk. Then she gave him a friendly pat on the side and turned laughing to Otto with an absolute torrent of words.

'Momma, she say you too big-a boy,' laughed Otto. 'She cuddle little-a shrimp and crab, but whales are as big-a . . . as-a big . . . as-a . . .' and he threw out two expressive arms.

'I know,' said Wilberforce, pretending to be hurt, 'as big as the Gasworks. You might think size was an advantage,' he went on with a twinkle in his eye, 'but don't you believe it! It's always the little'uns get the hugs.' And with a mock-tragic air, he broke into a lugubrious rumble:

> 'Nobody loves me! Everybody hates me!
> I'm going to the garden to eat worms!
> Long thin . . .'

But before he could finish the song, Momma reached up and gave him two great big kisses, one on each cheek, and Wilberforce went as red as a beetroot, and everybody laughed, and Wilberforce himself joined in.

Then, while Momma bustled off to get what Otto called 'a leetle-a snack,' they had time to look round. The cave started at the foot of the cliff well under water, and arched five or six feet above the surface. Melody and Nelson thought it was huge, but it looked a bit narrow to Wilberforce.

'I feel like an omnibus trying to get down a rabbit hole,' he said rather doubtfully, and then, 'Oh well, heave-ho!' with a wriggle and a flip of his great fluke tail, per-rump-ah—he was inside.

And the Blue Cave was almost magic, because by a trick of the light coming through the water everything that swam there seemed to be made of sapphire, while the sandy floor was turned to silver and every bubble in the water became a sparkling diamond.

'You look like two sapphire brooches,' said Wilberforce.

'It's Aladdin's cave,' cried Melody.

'*E bella*,' concluded Nelson.

'Already is-a speaking our language!' cried Otto delightedly and patted the little fellow on the back till he glowed with pride.

'Now I show-a you the view upstairs,' said Otto when at last they had taken it all in.

'Splendid idea,' said Wilberforce, 'I need a breath of fresh air.'

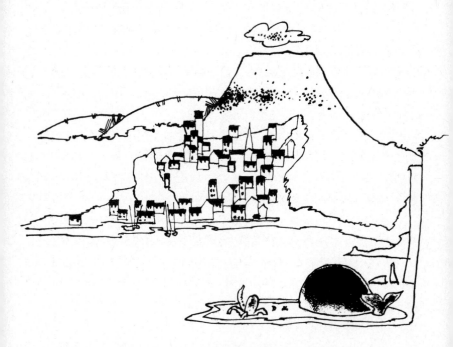

So they swam out again through the narrow opening and started an easy climb—blubble-ubble, obble-obble—up towards the surface, looking down as they went up on the 'garden' below. It was a gently shelving stretch of delightfully smooth sand, where clumps of branch-weed and feathery sea-fern swayed between rocks covered with flower-like anemones in water clear as crystal.

. . . Ibble-ebble, abble-abble, sfisch!—they surfaced. Nelson clambered onto Wilberforce's back, and Otto made a little lagoon with two of his arms for Melody to swim in.

'I don't known which is prettier,' she said 'inside the cave or outside.'

'I like *out*side best,' said Nelson. 'Inside it's like . . . like Buckingham Palace; it's so grand you're almost afraid of breaking something, but outside's where you can play and *do* things.'

Wilberforce and Otto laughed.

The island lay seaward of the bay where the ship had anchored. Once again they looked at the blue vista with white houses at sea level and the range of mountains flecked with snow in the hazy distance.

'Splendid view, all those mountains!' said Wilberforce. 'What's the big fellow all by himself, the one that looks as if he's had his peak cut off with the cloud on top?'

'Is-a no cloud, is-a smoke,' said Otto. 'Is-a the "Old Man"—the "Old Man" who "smoke-a the pipe."'

'The "Old Man" smoking his pipe?'

'*Si*, that is-a how we call him—the "Old Man". Is-a no mountain, is-a volcano, and when he "smoke-a his pipe", it means soon he go up, "boom"!'

'A volcano!' said Nelson with eyes like saucers.

'*Si*, a volcano! But here we all OK,' Otto reassured him. 'The "Old Man" is too far. Also I, Otto, am here and keep-a you safe. Nothing 'appen with Otto about.' And the little creature stuck out his chest and hammered on it with his fists.

'And when he goes up, what happens?' asked Nelson, still a little tremulous.

'Is-a *maestoso*, *superbo*! Good as fireworks, but better more twenty times.'

'Oh, I like fireworks,' said Nelson brightening up. 'Is it a very big "boom"? When will it go "boom" do you think? I do hope there are lots of coloured stars,' and he started to dance up and down with excitement. 'Will it go "boom" tonight?'

'Hey!' said Wilberforce, 'if you jump about like that, *you'll* go "boom" yourself—right up into the sky!'

Just then, they heard a voice below, and Otto cut in:

'Momma make-a the call. The leetle-a snack is-a ready.'

So they forgot all about volcanoes and dived — blabble-abble, ebble-ibble, obble-obble, ubble-ubble, oompf!—back to the garden. And there on a splendid white-topped marble table ('Roman remains!' said Melody, who had done a 'project' at school and so knew all about it), Momma had laid the 'leetle-a snack'—huge bowls of spaghetti made from special branch-weed flour with lashings of red leaf-weed sauce.

Wilberforce eyed his dish doubtfully. There are certain technical difficulties for a whale who wants to eat spaghetti. Otto, of course, sat down at once and twiddled the strands with practised assurance round a fork, which he could easily hold in his tentacles.

'Er—yes!' said Wilberforce watching him at work, and then, 'Quite so!' he added, seeing Nelson using a claw to give a fair imitation of Otto's fork management. And then, 'Well, fins were made before forks!' He put his great mouth down level with the plate in front of him and gave a little suck—slurp! One length of spaghetti slithered between his lips and disappeared—slick! Then there was another—slurp, slick! and a second strand vanished.

'Nothing to it!' murmured Wilberforce with satisfaction, and—slurp, slick! slurp, slick!—the strands of spaghetti vanished one by one.

But for Wilberforce, who had a relatively large appetite, it seemed rather slow work, and so presently he took several strands at once and gave a slightly larger 'slurp', though of course he was trying not to make too much noise for fear of seeming rude. Unfortunately the 'slurp' wasn't quite a big enough 'slurp', and only half the spaghetti disappeared, leaving Wilberforce with a fringe of white strands round his chin.

'Oh dear!' he muttered, 'I must look like Father Christmas.'

Of course Wilberforce didn't want to draw attention to himself with a larger 'slurp' still, so he flipped the mouthful upwards and gulped. All was well except for the longest strand, which brushed against his nose and stuck.

'Ha, er-ha, er-ha!'—Wilberforce started to sneeze, it tickled so. 'Ha, er-ha, er-ha!' The tickle got quite out of control, and then, 'Ha-choo!' he sneezed. And when a whale sneezes, he SNEEZES. So everything on the table was joggled and spilt. 'Ha-choo!' he gave another devastating sneeze. And this time, he not only upset everything, but also caught his chin on the corner of the marble slab.

Poor Wilberforce was quite put out, what with his awful sneeze, and the hurt on his chin (which really was very painful). Tears started to his eyes, and he had to be very brave indeed to get out,

'Oh, I *am* sorry!'

But at once Otto was on one side of him, and kindly old Momma was on the other.

'Is-a no matter, old friend, is-a no matter at all. The spaghetti, she is very slippery.'

And even as he was speaking, Momma had put a comforting bladder-locks dressing on the nasty little cut, and two of Otto's arms had cleared the table while two others had re-polished it, and the last four were quickly ladelling more spaghetti into fresh bowls quicker than a whole army of waiters.

'Now . . . we all-a happy?' asked Otto as they settled down again. 'You all say, please, "I happy!"'

'I happy!' everyone echoed.

'Is-a holiday time,' cried Otto, conducting.

'Is holiday time!' they all shouted back together, and everyone began to laugh and talk nineteen to the dozen, and Momma showed her white teeth in pleasure, and bowls were filled and refilled, till at last the meal was over, and Otto asked what they would like to do.

'I shall help Momma,' said Melody and went straight to where the little old lady was clearing the table. Momma, she felt, was the sort of person you could make immediate friends with, and tell anything to, even if you *couldn't* understand what she said in reply.

'I should like to go and explore, please,' cried Nelson excitedly.

'Is-a good! I also like the explore,' replied Otto with enthusiasm. 'We make the explore together!'

'As for me,' yawned Wilberforce, eyeing a particularly inviting bed of green leaf-weed, 'after that very splendid meal, for me, my energetic little playmates—a little nap,' and he ambled over and settled down on the luxuriant mattress. Then, noticing that he was now all alone, he set to work on a 'rune':

> 'Leg of toad and wing of bat,
> Make a new and natty hat . . .

mm-mm-mm . . . something shady, please.'

Then—plop!—and there he was in a huge Mexican sombrero with a brim as big as a cartwheel. This he pulled well over his eyes to keep out the sun, and with an 'mm-mm-mm, yes . . . very comfortable . . . mm-mm-mm . . .' he was soon '. . . mm-mm-mm . . .' fast asleep.

5

Nelson's Narrow Squeak

So Nelson and Otto set off to explore with Otto —schiff-fusz, schiff-fusz—in the lead.

'We go to the most best beach with-a rock and little-a pools of so interest and excite as-a you never see,' said Otto waving enthusiastic arms in all directions.

'Oh, I can't wait,' cried Nelson excitedly darting here and there with busy sideways shuffles that stirred up little puffs of sand wherever he walked on the sea-bed. And a whole colony of mussels shut up their shells in surprise and alarm—click-click-click, click, click-click— as he came upon them unexpectedly clustered on a large rock.

'Please-a to take-a the care 'ow-a u go!' said the biggest mussel through a slit in shell, and then he shut up shop—click—like the rest of them.

'Oh, *scusa*!' said Nelson, who was rapidly picking up the language.

Just then he spotted a skate-purse on the sand.

'Now I'm a great explorer,' he cried, tying it on his back like a knapsack.

'And I am your-a faithful bearer,' laughed Otto, falling in with the game.

'If we meet any hostile natives we shall have to defend ourselves till the Foreign Legion arrives,' Nelson went on heroically.

'Is all-a friendly, the natives in these-a parts,' Otto assured him.

But at that very moment, almost as if in contradiction, a deep drumming sound—boing! . . . boing! . . . boing!—came from the direction of the shore in a steady threatening rhythm.

'Drums!' cried Nelson, his eyes popping out of his head. 'Native war drums!'

'Is all-a friendly, the natives,' Otto repeated, 'all-a laugh and-a sing all the time.'

'Then perhaps it's a big Palaver. Perhaps they've heard we're coming and the natives are beating their drums to welcome Great Crab Effend and his mighty War Lord of the Eight Arms. I'm going to explore,' and he set off purposefully up the sandy incline and through the shallow, lace-like ripples on the beach.

'Have-a the care,' Otto called after him, 'on-a beach is-a *pericoloso*, danger from all sorts.'

But Nelson was out of hearing and had just scuttled through the last tiny ripples on to dry land.

Boing! . . . boing! . . . boing!—The noise was louder than ever, and there, a little way up the warm, grey, gritty beach, a small boy and his sister were bouncing up and down on a trampoline. Nelson had never seen one before.

'I say, what fun!' he cried as the little girl rose gracefully into the air pretending to fly with her arms. 'Oo-oo-oo!' he went on as the boy did a half-somersault to land on his back and shoot upright again from the springy canvas.

'I wish I could do that,' said the little crab, and then he spotted a big sandcastle which the two children had made just by the trampoline. To you and me, of course, it would have looked quite an ordinary sandcastle, but to Nelson it was Mount Everest, and that was the place for the best view.

So off he went, full of determination. 'Oof!' he panted after the first nine inches, and then 'Oo-er—dash!' he slithered half way back again. 'Crumbs!' he puffed some moments later, 'this is a vertiginous and practically precipitous ascent!' But, 'Excelsior!' he meant to get to the top, and by dint of much heaving and puffing and determined pulling and hauling, at last he reached the summit, or what he *thought* was the summit. For as he made the last triumphant heave, he found himself not on a mountain peak but . . . staring down into the crater of a volcano!

'Oh golly, oh crikey, oh Christopher Columbus!' he gasped, teetering on the very lip. 'Oo-oo-er! Er-ooh-er-ooh-er!' he chattered, with frantic claws circling to keep his balance. 'Er-ooh-er-ooh-er-ooh-er!' he cried again as all his legs but one started waving wildly. Then—bomp!—down he fell into the dreaded crater, head over heels, to land flat on his back. And there poor Nelson lay, legs and claws kicking in the air, and quite unable to turn himself over.

What if the volcano started to 'smoke its pipe'! What if it should go 'boom' while Nelson was lying there helpless on his back! For the poor little fellow quite thought he was in a *real* volcano.

'He-e-lp!' he cried feebly.

But nobody heard him, because the children had got tired of jumping about and had gone off

to play higher up the beach, and there was no other living thing in sight except a small sand hopper, who hopped—ping!—onto Nelson's nose and—ping!—off again without so much as a 'Can I take a message to someone for you?'

'He-e-lp!' Nelson cried again and again.

Now Otto may have been a rather flamboyant young octopus and even rather boastful, but nobody could possibly say that he wasn't thoughtful and considerate, and he was a little worried about Nelson being on the beach. 'Is-a *pericoloso*—danger from all-a sorts,' as he had said. So every two or three minutes a small round head bobbed up through the inshore ripples, just to keep an eye on things, and one of these bobs fortunately coincided with Nelson's fifth cry for help.

Otto bobbed up and down frantically to try and locate the cry, but it was a moment or two before he spotted the tips of two agitated claws waving above the lip of the crater, and realised what had happened. But how could an octopus get across the dry sand above the water line? Otto looked round and saw a large pumice rock well anchored to the sea bed but just sticking up above the water, and it gave him an idea.

First he pulled himself above the surface and shouted as loudly as he could, 'Have-a no fear, Nelson, my little-a friend; Otto is 'ere: is all-a well. I rescue you, but first I go to make-a some arrangement. Soon I come back!'

And off he shot like a little comet—schiff-fusz, schiff-fusz, schiff-fusz—propelling himself jetwise across the bay.

Back in the garden he found Wilberforce fast asleep on his mattress of green leaf-weed.

'Ou-ilberforz-a, wake-a, wake-a!' Otto cried hammering on the whale's great back with all eight arms together.

'Um-um-um! . . . What is it?' said Wilberforce, waking up suddenly. 'I was just in the middle of my beauty sleep!'

'Is-a no time for the sleeping beauty,' cried Otto 'Nelson is in danger. Has-a fallen in the crater of a volcano!'

'What!' exclaimed Wilberforce, starting up so violently that he knocked his sombrero off, 'and the "Old Man" smoking his pipe!'

'Is-a not a real volcano. Is-a sand volcano made by the *bambini*, the children. But on his-a back is Nelson and is impossible for 'im to climb out.'

At that, the great fluke tail was at work—per-rump-ah, per-rump-ah, per-rump-ah—and they were on their way. A minute or so later they were back at the rock opposite the trampoline. Otto fastened four of his arms firmly round it and gripped Wilberforce's tail with the rest.

'Now,' he cried, 'swim out-a to sea. Swim-a so 'ard as you can!'

So Wilberforce started swimming, and Otto's arms began to stretch, and they stre-etched, and they stre-e-etched, and they stre-e-e-etched like elastic, and for poor Otto it was very painful, but he held on till the last possible moment. Then he cried,

'Now I let-a go,' and as the four arms on one side released their hold on Wilberforce, the four round the rock fired him like a catapult straight towards the trampoline.

'Help-a she come!' cried Otto as he skimmed through the air. 'Reach-a your claws up, up, Nelson! . . . The landing she is-a now . . . four-a, . . . three-a . . . two-a . . . one-a!' and on the 'one', Nelson reached up and Otto reached down, and their hands joined like two acrobats between trapezes in a circus. Then—boing!— Otto hit the trampoline, and—whee-ee-ee-ee-ee—out they zoomed safely back to sea, where Wilberforce was waiting with his big, warm, friendly grin.

'Look, Wilberforce,' cried Nelson, 'I'm flying! Otto, you're the parachute, and I'm the space capsule.'

Then there was a great big splash, and a second later the three friends were dancing ring-a-ring-of-roses in the water with delight.

'Oh, Otto thank you; you are clever,' cried Nelson.

'*Prego*! Not to mention! Is-a nothing,'

replied Otto nonchalantly, 'such-a waves of the brain, I have them twenty times the day.'

And so they set off home gently and comfortably with Nelson riding on Wilberforce's back—per-rump-ah, per-rump-ah.

'Oh,' said Nelson, 'I *do* hope we can have an adventure like that every day.'

'*Per favore*, if you please!' said Otto waving his tentacles stiffly, 'not unless you will kindly buy me a new set of arms!'

6

The 'Old Man' Blows His Top

It was after breakfast some mornings later. Momma had promised to make Melody a head-scarf like her own, and they had both gone off to a special seaweed bed to choose the material. Nelson had clambered up to a convenient ledge on the rock at the corner of the garden, as he had taken to doing every morning recently, to see if the 'Old Man' was 'smoking his pipe'.

Today, one grey plume of smoke had scarcely faded away before another puffed up out of the crater and took its place. Nelson put his head below the water to give Wilberforce the news.

'That's six puffs of smoke from the "Old Man" since breakfast,' he called.

'My, my!' said Wilberforce opening one eye. He was stretched in a hammock made from the red and white spinnaker of a passing yacht, which he had slung between two convenient rocks. 'Six puffs, did you say? Well, well!' and he turned over to go back to sleep.

'But SIX puffs since breakfast! That means he may go "boom" at any moment!' cried Nelson, exasperated at the great whale's lack of interest.

'Up there—possibly! Down here, as old Otto puts it, "not-a to worry!"' And Wilberforce sighed contentedly as his hammock rocked in the gentle swell. 'This is the life, my sandy little Sinbad,' he murmured, tilting his sombrero. '*Dolce far niente*, as they say—whatever that means.'

'It means you're jolly lazy,' said Nelson impatiently. And indeed, the bright sun and warm water seemed to have turned his big friend into a regular old lazy-bones.

'And what better place to be lazy in?' yawned Wilberforce, staring idly up at the bright saffron keel of a jade-green rowing boat which was dipping leisurely through the mirror surface above him, its long flat-bladed sweeps leaving a line of crystal circles in their wake.

Schiff-up!—'Is-a the luverly morning! And what-a we do today?' broke in Otto's cheery voice, as he came round the corner of the

garden laden with packages from the market.

'What about trying to swim right round the island?' suggested Nelson, full of enthusiasm.

'Or on the other hand, my dashing little dynamos,' murmured Wilberforce, 'what about just lying here and admiring this splendid view?'

'Ou-ilberforz-a, you are so lazy as a dormouse,' laughed Otto; and then to Nelson, 'What-a we do with this lazy whale-y?'

'Let's tip him out of his hammock,' Nelson suggested.

So he and Otto put their shoulders against the whale's great side.

'One, two, three, pu-u-ush,' cried Nelson, and they pushed, and they pu-ushed, and they pu-u-u-ushed, but they might just as well have tried to push over the Houses of Parliament.

Wilberforce laughed and rumbled:

> 'Yo-ho, heave-ho!
> Yo-ho, heave-ho!
> Pom, pom, pom-tiddle-om . . .'

'Come on!' he teased them, 'You aren't trying. Pu-ush, my little seaside steamrollers!'

'Let's try shaking him out instead,' said Nelson.

And then a very odd thing happened—the hammock started to shake by itself. It was only a little quiver at first, but then it became a tremor, and the tremor became a wild quake, and it wasn't only the hammock that was quaking, but the rocks and the sea-bed as well. Suddenly there was a sharp 'crack' like a gun going off at point blank range, and this was followed by a growling rumble as if six express trains were all crossing a steel bridge together.

'The "Old Man",' shouted Otto above the terrifying din, 'is-a going "boom"!'

Per-roosh!—They darted upwards to the surface by Nelson's look-out. The sight that met their eyes was awe-inspiring.

Over on the mainland, the volcano belched a solid black pillar of smoke, tinged red above the crater with reflected fire. Up into the air it rose, a mighty pall, higher and higher until a cross current of wind caught it in the upper atmosphere and turned it out to sea, straight in their direction.

The awful rumble grew steadily in intensity. As they watched, fascinated, with another 'crack' the lip of the crater crumbled, and boiling lava like red-hot porridge started to ooze inexorably down the volcano's side.

Out to sea, the jade-green rowing boat was pulling for dear life across wind to escape the pall of smoke. But already the people on board were having to cover their heads with boxes, trays, a thwart from the boat itself—anything they could find to shield them from the angry black cloud which blotted out the sun and rained down grit, and pebbles, and stones, and even rocks along its path.

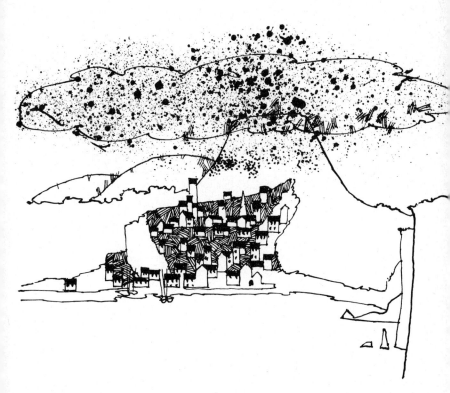

And now there were spouts of spray as the stones hit the sea—plop-ish-sh, plop-ish-sh! —and they could almost hear the hiss as the water dowsed the red-hot cinders.

Fortunately their island lay out beyond the smoke's dark track, but only by a short distance. The friends watched spell-bound.

'I'm glad our island's so far off shore,' said Nelson at last, as the rowing boat reached the safety of a neighbouring beach.

'*Si*,' replied Otto, 'is-a very angry, the "Old Man".'

Suddenly Wilberforce had an awful thought. 'Momma! Melody!' he exclaimed, 'They're in the middle of it! The seaweed bed's out there!' And he pointed to where the sea was leaping under its hail of pumice rocks.

'Momma, she know,' reassured Otto. 'Must-a swim only under shade of big-a rock; is all-a well then.'

Wilberforce's fluke tail flicked with doubt for a moment. Then,

'I expect you're right, Otto old man, but I'd like to make sure,' he announced.

'Me too,' said Nelson.

'Is-a good so. I show you the way,' agreed the octopus.

So — per-rump-ah, per-rump-ah — they started on a long shallow dive out to sea. A minute later they were in the danger zone. Plop-ish-sh, plop-ish-sh, plop-ish-sh—the hot cinders sizzled around them, mostly mere pebbles, but some as big as cricket balls, and every now and then, one as big as your head. Of course, under water they were cooled and slowed down, but it was not a comfortable situation, especially for small crabs and even young octopuses.

'Take cover, you two,' cried Wilberforce in his 'emergency voice', 'underneath me, and then we'll dive as deep as we can.'

On the bottom Wilberforce started moving steadily in order to shelter his two young friends while picking his way as best he could to avoid the bits of lava that were still sinking around him.

At the edge of the seaweed bed they stopped and started to call.

'Melody!' shouted Wilberforce.

'Momma!' echoed Otto.

But there was no reply. They swam forward a little and called again . . . and again . . . and again, and they were all beginning to get really worried when suddenly Wilberforce stopped.

'Sh-sh-sh!' he said.

In between the plops of falling stones they could hear, a little way off, a voice. It was a very talkative voice, and it was a laughing and friendly voice, and it was Momma's voice, jabbering away nineteen to the dozen as it always did, with chuckles and laughs in every pause.

Per-roosh!—they all dashed forward. On the far side of a very big rock, in a small sandy bay, they came upon Melody and Momma surrounded by snippets and lengths of seaweed of all colours and textures and sizes, and patterns and threads were littered everywhere.

'The red's very nice,' Melody was saying as they swam up, 'and of course the golden-brown is very pretty. . . . I can't make my mind up . . . and that green would show up my coral clasp beautifully . . .'

'Melody! Momma! Are you all right?' cried Wilberforce.

'Why, where have you swum from?' replied Melody. 'Of course we're all right. Momma's going to make my head scarf as soon as I can decide on the colour.'

Momma nodded and laughed a fat, friendly, jolly laugh of agreement.

'But didn't you feel the shake?' asked Nelson.

'And the big bang?' added Wilberforce.

'And the old-a rumble-a-grumble,' concluded Otto.

'What bang? What rumble?' Melody turned to Momma, who gave a great shrug with her fins and a laughing agreement that it was beyond her understanding.

And then the three friends realised that the rocks and stones weren't coming down any more. They had swum right across the shadow of the smoke cloud and come out on the far side where they were safe under a clear sky again. Momma and Melody had been so busy talking and choosing materials that they hadn't felt a thing.

'What's all this about bangs and tremors?' Melody went on.

'It's the "Old Man",' cried Nelson, 'he's going "boom", and he's very angry!'

'What!' cried Melody, 'the "Old Man" going "boom" and you never told us? You old meanies!'

Wilberforce coughed, and then, '. . . Well, well!' he murmured.

'To please the *signorina* all-a the time is-a not possible' shrugged Otto.

And Otto looked at Nelson, and Nelson looked at Wilberforce, and Wilberforce looked into the middle distance, and suddenly everybody burst out laughing.

'Oh, Wilberforce, of course I see now,' cried Melody. 'You came to make sure we were safe. How kind of you! And oh, *poor* Wilberforce! Look at those bumps and bruises on your back; how *did* you come by them?'

'Oh, that doesn't matter,' answered the whale, 'now that we know you're all right.'

So Momma picked up some of each of the seaweeds that she thought Melody might like, and they all swam up to the surface—blubble-ubble, obble-obble, ibble-ebble, abble-abble-sfisch. The 'Old Man' was smoking as hard as ever but the rumbles had died down, and the wind had changed so that the black cloud was now blowing right away from them and out to sea.

After watching for a little longer, they all turned and swam for home with Melody and Nelson taking it in turns to have a pig-a-back ride with Otto, as poor old Wilberforce was rather sore from all the stones that had tumbled on him. Momma murmured soothingly and put on warm sand poultices as they went along.

Nelson said, 'Terrifying! I wouldn't have missed it for the world!'

And Otto said, '*E vero maestoso!* Magnificent!'

And Wilberforce said, 'It was terrific! A truly enormous and effervescent effluxion!'

'Yes,' said Melody, with a look of deep concentration on her face, 'I think I shall choose the pink one.'

7

Wilberforce to the Rescue

Wilberforce was floating comfortably on a bank of branch weed, and as the early sun filtered down through the warm, clear sea, he was discussing with himself the important question of whether it was better to be rather lazy and half awake or *really* lazy and half asleep? Doubtfully he opened one eye, and just as he did so Nelson scuttled out from behind a rock crying;

'Bang! Bang, bang, bang! You're dead.'

'Good gracious me!' laughed Wilberforce starting up. 'Please don't do that again without warning. You nearly frightened me out of my skin.' Then, seeing the small cap pistol which Nelson was brandishing in one claw, he added, 'And what have you got there, my gun-toting little stickleback?'

'It's my six-shooter,' replied Nelson proudly.

'It fell over the side of a pleasure boat while I was playing out by the big rocks. It's made for caps really, but I use the bobbles from the bladder-wrack and they work just as well. . . . Hallo, Otto,' he added as the cheerful young octopus shot—schiff-fusz, schiff-fusz—round the corner of the cove with a net of fresh green-leaf weed which he had just been gathering for Momma's larder.

'And the good-a morning to you, my leetle-a crab friend, and to my big-a friend, Ouilberforz-a. Is-a all the good news this morning; the "Old Man" no more he "smoke-a his pipe".'

'Oh, splendid!' exclaimed Wilberforce, because for a whole week black smoke and lava had continued to pour from the volcano, and although the wind had blown steadily on-shore, they had felt it safest not to stray too far from home. 'That's first rate; now we can go and explore somewhere new.'

'*Si!*' replied Otto enthusiastically. 'Today we cross to mainland. I take-a you the good place for the pic-a-nic-a, *molto buono*.'

'Oh!' said Nelson, and there was a questioning note in his voice. 'You don't think the "Old Man" may go "boom" again?'

'The "Old-a Man" he has gone-a back to sleep,' Otto tried to reassure him.

'Oh!' said Nelson, and the doubtful note in his voice was now unmistakable.

'Wouldn't you *like* a picnic somewhere new?' asked Wilberforce.

'Well,' said Nelson, scraping the sand with a disappointed foot, 'well, I *had* rather hoped that *someone*,' and he glanced at Wilberforce, 'would play "Cowboys and Indians" with me and my new six-shooter.'

'But that's easy,' smiled the whale kindly, 'we'll do *both*. We'll be cowboys on the journey there and back, and have the picnic in between whiles, eh Otto?'

'Oh, goody-goody-goody! Bang-bang-bang-bang-bang-bang!' and Nelson blazed off all six rounds from his revolver in sheer excitement.

'But please not-a to shoot Otto into little-a pieces before the game-a begin,' laughed the octopus.

'Oh, *scusa*!' said Nelson politely.

'*Prego*, not-a to mention!' smiled Otto.

'So that's settled,' said Wilberforce, 'Now, what say, pardner, you mosey over to the cook-house and ask Miss Melody to rustle up some grub?'

Nelson was off to the kitchen long before Wilberforce had finished. '. . . And we're going to have an explore to the mainland,' he said, 'and we're going to play "Cowboys and Indians" all the way over, and I'm going to shoot everyone with my new pistol, and please, Wilberforce says can you make us the picnic?'

Well, Momma was so delighted when Otto explained, that she started talking not nineteen but thirty-eight to the dozen, and of course Melody agreed to help too. When Nelson and Otto got back to the garden, Wilberforce had recited one of Aunty Barnacle's runes and was wearing a forty-gallon Stetson cowboy hat. Not to be outdone, Otto tied a length of ribbon weed round his head and stuck two seagull feathers in the back.

'Me, Big-a Chief Eight-Foot,' he said.

Soon Momma appeared carrying a large basket covered with a white cloth in which there were lots of tantalising bulges, suggesting a real picnic of favourite things when appetites had been sharpened by games and 'explores' later in the day. Melody was wearing her new head scarf and a matching apron just like Momma's but in pink feathery Bryopsis, and everyone said how pretty she looked.

So they set out—per-rump-ah, per-rump-ah —with Wilberforce bucking and bronching like a metalsome mustang for Nelson to ride on, while Otto galloped round and round with blood-curdling war cries—hoo-woo-hoo-woo-hoo—waving pretend tomahawks and firing bows and arrows with all his arms together so that he was not so much an Indian brave as a whole tribe of Comanches setting out on the warpath.

Nelson took cover under the forty-gallon stetson and shot everything in sight till they were dead three or four times over—bang-bang, bang-bang-bang—and some things like a large skate that flip-flopped by were turned into 'positively perforated pepper-pots.' Wilberforce lent local colour by rumbling:

> 'Home, home on the range,
> Where the eel and the halibut play,
> Tiddle-om-ti-pom-pom. . . .'

Momma and Melody swam quietly along behind with the picnic basket—pfut-pfut-pfut—and its mouth-watering bulges—pfut-pfut-pfut—laughing and talking and talking and laughing, and entirely unconcerned by the horribly gory struggle going on all round them.

Well, of course, with all the excitement of the battle, it seemed no time at all before the sand started to shelve upwards again, and Otto called,

'Is-a the good-a place to 'alt.'

Momma flopped down with the basket beside her and started to fan herself with a large frond of branch weed, and everyone else floated up to the surface—blubble-ubble, obble-obble, ibble-ebble, abble-abble, sfisch—to look at the view on top.

How the weather had changed! Whispy grey clouds were starting to gather on the peaks of the mountains, which now seemed much nearer than before, and as they surfaced a sudden puff of quite cold wind caught Wilberforce's cowboy hat and whirled it out to sea. The Stetson landed on its brim, which almost immediately filled with water. Presently a claw wavered up from its under side, felt for a foothold, took a firm grip of the band . . . and up struggled Nelson.

'Sorry I couldn't save your hat for you, Wilberforce,' he called, clambering over the curly bit. 'I held on, but the wind was too strong for me.'

He scuttled up to the peak of the forty-gallon stetson's crown.

'Hey! This is my castle,' he went on, 'and that,' pointing to the water-logged brim, 'is the moat. Hey, Melody, come and swim in my moat!' And with a little help, Melody kindly obliged.

While all this was going on, things in the world about them were changing very rapidly. A cold wind started to blow, the clouds swept down from the mountains suddenly obscuring the sun, and before anyone realised what had happened, Melody and Nelson found themselves right out at sea with a whistling wind and a cold douche of rain. Then . . . the hat-castle started to move in a great big circle.

'Woops!' cried Nelson as he lost grip and tumbled down into the 'moat'. 'It's a bit round-and-round for my tum.'

'It's making me feel giddy,' said Melody, looking around nervously.

And then it seemed that the clouds stooped out of the sky and picked up a thread of sea to form a whirling column of water like a pillar from cloud to wave. Three other pillars formed themselves in quick succession, one behind the other, and the hat began to circle faster and faster round the leading pillar, which sucked them menacingly nearer and nearer to its whirling, roaring vortex.

In-shore, their friends suddenly became aware of what was happening.

'Is-a the water spouts!' cried Otto. '*Molto pericoloso*—much-a the danger!'

For a moment, Wilberforce watched aghast. It was clear that if the hat was drawn into the seething centre of the hurricane it would be battered to pieces with both its occupants.

At once the giant fluke tail thrashed—per-rump-ah, per-rump-ah, per-rump-ah—but by the time Wilberforce had reached the first spout, the hat was over on the far side. There was only one thing to do. With all his speed and strength, the great whale swam for the very centre of the spout itself, and at the last minute leapt out of the water to hit it right in the middle crash!—cutting it in two. Then—splash!—he landed with a grunt. Looking back he saw that his plan had worked, and the broken spout had subsided. But still the hat was out of reach, and two more spouts marched like black giants towards them. Twice again, but each time with flagging energy, Wilberforce charged and leapt and broke them in two.

And now at last Wilberforce found himself near the hat and was able to take hold of the brim with his mouth and start, tired and breathless, to swim away from the ominous advance of the last whirling tornado. But weakened as he was, and with the stetson as a new encumbrance, the howling giant seemed to be bearing down on them and coming ever nearer. Then, little by little, the gap started to widen again. Wilberforce was making ground.

'Go on, Wilberforce,' Melody encouraged him, 'We're nearly there.'

'I don't think I can last much longer,' he gasped through clenched teeth.

'You can, you can!' urged Melody.

'I will, I will!' the whale responded. But in the very act of his speaking, the hat slipped from his mouth, spilling Melody and Nelson into the sea beside him. For a moment all three were struck with terror lest they be sucked back into the hurricane.

But then, as suddenly as it had blown up, the wind changed course, the cyclone disappeared, and like a trick of stage lighting the sun and the blue sky returned, bright as ever, and the friends were left panting on the unruffled surface.

'*E superbo!*' cried Otto swimming up, and patting the whale on the back.

'Momma she cry with both her eyes to see you so heroical, my mighty Ou-ilberforz-a.'

> 'Through rain and through hail,
>   In the teeth of the gale,
>   Who came to our rescue?
>   Wilberforce Whale!'

'Thank you,' said Wilberforce, still panting. 'I'm afraid I'm a bit out of training . . . ought to have been able to break up all four of those spouts . . . too much of that delicious spaghetti! . . . shall have to put myself on a diet!'

'Diet? Pfui! Such-a strength you must keep up with good eatings,' said Otto. 'So, Momma, she 'ave the glorious pic-a-nic-a ready. Come, we go!'

'Wait a mo',' said Wilberforce. 'What happened to my cowboy hat?'

'I'm afraid that's a total marine disaster,' replied Nelson, looking out to sea at a distant battered lump of felt which swayed soggily on the easing waves. 'Look!' he added as the hat finally started to sink, 'it's the wreck of the forty-gallon Stetson.'

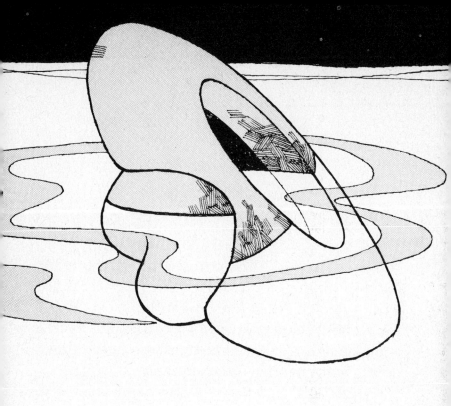

'But all hands were saved, thanks to Wilberforce,' added Melody.

'And now,' said Otto as the hat gave a last
'glup!' and disappeared, 'now for Momma's
pic-a-nic-a.' So—blabble-abble, ebble-ibble,
obble-obble, ubble-ubble, oomf—they all swam
down.

8

The Grand Gala Night

Momma clearly had exciting news as she bustled in from market some days later. Her torrent of words started when she was still out by the big rock and became an absolute Niagara by the time she plumped her net of purchases down on the sand near the marble table.

Schiff-fusz, schiff-up—Otto shot over and joined in her excitement.

'Is-a the regatta 'istorical,' he cried delightedly. 'The *festa* with decorated boats. They announce to Momma at market. Is-a most jolly. It all 'appen next Friday!'

'That's our last day here,' said Wilberforce. 'It'll make a splendid ending to our stay.'

'What's a historical regatta?' asked Nelson.

'Is-a the parade of boats with costume,' replied Otto, 'for the ricordo of most 'istorical affair. You like I tell?'

'Oh, please,' said Melody.

'Was-a long time ago,' Otto began, 'and this lord of our island have-a the *argomento* with this other lord across the sea. So they decide to make-a the battle together. So this first, he sail across the sea to the *castello* of this other one, and he blow 'is trump—plah-ha! plah-ha!— and who come out on the . . . how you call that up there of the *castello*?'

'Battlements,' suggested Melody.

'*Si!* Oo come out on the battlements but the other lord's little-a daughter—most beautiful is this little-a daughter, *e una principessa vera*— you understand?'

'She is a real princess,' cried Nelson.

Otto nodded. 'The first one, he see the so beautiful principessa, and is struck by love like-a the thunderbolt. "*Bellissima!*" he cry, "We will not 'ave the battle after all. I will marry the *principessa* instead; I love her very big!" And they make the procession of boats to bring the so beautiful *principessa* back with much happy-makings. Now, once the year we 'ave the 'istorical regatta to remember by with the beeg-a parade of boats, and after there is the dancing and the fireworks.'

'Oh, how romantic!' exclaimed Melody.

87

'Fireworks?' asked Nelson hopefully.

'*Si*,' Otto replied, 'after the regatta the dancing and the fireworks, and all dress up to welcome the *principessa*.'

'Decorated boats and dressing up!' murmured Wilberforce. 'Hm . . . yes . . . perhaps . . . yes, I think so! . . . Yes, indeed, why not?'

And from that moment his whole character seemed to change. He spent the rest of the day hidden behind a big rock, and if anybody asked him to come out and play, he answered, 'Go away, I'm busy!' And even Momma's calls for 'Leetle-a snacks' were greeted with 'Please! I'm just in the middle!' And from then onwards, all that any of his friends saw or heard of him was a muted mutter from his hide-out:

'"Tail of whiting, . . . er . . . fin of hake," . . .

yes not bad!

"See what costume you can make!"

No that won't work. How about:

"Abra-cad-abra and fee-fi-fo-fum,
What sort of rune makes a fancy dress come?"

88

No?... Well, what about...'

And so the mutterings went on and on, and sometimes he just lay in deep thought, and at others he would suddenly put out his head and call;

'Can anybody think of a rhyme for "Oceanographic"?'

'Wilberforce!' exclaimed Melody.

'I think you're barmy,' said Nelson.

But Wilberforce didn't mind. He didn't even seem to hear, and just went back to his absentminded mutterings.

And then, early on the last morning, he suddenly burst out with, 'I've got it!... I've got it! I've got it! I've got it!' and wild with excitement he shot straight up through the water like a rocket—per-roosh—with a great swirl. 'Hooray! I've got it!' he cried, doing a loop-the-loop.

'Whatever is it all about?' asked Melody.

'Oh-ho, never you mind, my shrimpy little reveller. You just wait and see!'

'Oh please tell us what it is,' begged Nelson, 'I hate secrets and having to wait.'

But Wilberforce was adamant and said nothing, and it wasn't until they were all getting ready to go and watch the parade of boats, that they suddenly realised that he had disappeared. Just when he had gone, no one could say, because they had all been very busy over preparations, but it was certain that *now* he was nowhere to be found.

'Well, *I* can't think where he has got to,' said Nelson returning from his third unsuccessful search of the Blue Cave. 'You don't think he's hiding because he doesn't want to go home,' he added. 'I mean, it's our last whole day . . . I wish we didn't have to go!'

'Wilberforce wouldn't do anything so silly,' said Melody. 'Anyhow you've got the fireworks to look forward to.'

'Then he must have got lost,' said Nelson.

'You can't lose anything as big as Wilber-force,' Melody replied. 'He isn't exactly a needle in a haystack, is he?'

'Not unless you had a very *big* haystack,' agreed Nelson.

'Is-a for me like the conjuror and the lady which disappear,' put in Otto. 'Hey presto! There she is! And hey presto! There she isn't!' And he gave a theatrical wave with his arms.

At that moment Melody noticed a piece of white planking from the side of a stove-in dinghy, lying on the marble table. It had very large, round, purple crayon lettering on it.

'How silly of us not to see it before,' she cried. 'Look! Wilberforce has left a note . . . it says, "Don't wait for me. See you at the *festa*. Love, W." Well, that's a relief,' she laughed.

'Then, *andiamo*,' cried Nelson, 'let's go! We don't want to miss anything.'

'*Pronto!* At once, I show the way,' cried Otto and led off with Momma towards the island's harbour, where scores of boats were drawn up in two lines with a wide lane in between. Down below, fishes of all colours and shapes and sizes were arriving by shoals—sfish-sfash-sfish —to join in the celebration. Most of them, of course, would have to be content to look upwards and watch the keels pass overhead, but Otto could just float level with the surface and make a little lagoon with two arms for Melody and Momma to swim in while Nelson, as usual, clambered on top of his head.

They had spent so much time looking for Wilberforce that the first boat was just going by as they took up their places. It was all gold and white and was rowed by thirty-two oars. Every rower was in blue livery, while on the poop astern under a canopy decorated with golden lilies there were people dressed in medieval costume representing the ambassador of France and his court. Then there was a yellow boat with red dragons from China, and a green boat with crescent moons from Turkey, and everybody dressed up in such bright and colourful clothes as you never did see. So the boats rowed by from all the countries of the world, and the onlookers cheered and laughed and waved. The people on board laughed and waved back.

At last the biggest boat of all came into sight, and this one was rowed by *sixty-four* oars. It was all silver and white with lilac awnings, and under the awnings, surrounded by her maids of honour, stood the little princess, as pretty as a picture and all in her bridal robes. As she approached smiling and waving to either side, the cheers swelled and swelled. But it was not for the boat, or even for the little *principessa* that the cheers rose. It was to the bow of the ship that all eyes turned.

'*Guarda*! Look!' everyone called. For where the bow cut the waves there leapt and frolicked a huge fish dressed in a suit of pure silver scales with a crown of gold and diamonds on his head. A great leather collar set with purple amethysts lay round his neck, and from this, two silver chains led back to the boat as if he were drawing it along. And as he swam he leapt like a porpoise as if to say, 'I am a special royal fish in the service of the beautiful *principessa!*' Everybody shouted and cheered with delight.

'*Bravo! Bravissimo!*' they called, and it was partly for the little princess and partly for Wilberforce, because, of course, that is who the great 'fish' was.

'Well, I never!' exclaimed Melody. 'So *that's* what he's been doing all this time— making up a new magic rune!'

'It must have been an absolutely super-duper rune,' echoed Nelson, and Otto summed it up:

'*E superbo!* Never 'ave I seen such!'

Well, that is really the end of the holiday except that, as Otto had promised, there was a great party that evening in the Blue Cave, and it seemed that every fish for miles around was there. Otto became a complete band in himself and played half a dozen instruments all at once. And Wilberforce danced the polka with Momma till they were both quite out of breath, and Momma laughed and wobbled with delight. Nelson did a sword dance round a pair of scissors that he found, and Melody was in

endless demand with a whole succession of partners, particularly a delightful family of little *scampi*. Then Wilberforce and Otto sang a duet:

   '*Funiculi-funicula! Funiculi-funicula!*
   Pom-ti tiddle, ay-di-ho, di-dum, di-dum, di-dah!'

By this time it had grown quite dark, so they all swam out and surfaced comfortably by Nelson's look-out rock to watch the fireworks.

Sh-sh-sh-sh-sh, bang, clo-clo-clo-clop, went the rockets, and fish-wish-wish-wish-wish went the catherine wheels, and everybody said 'Oh-oh!' and 'Ah-ah-ah!' And Nelson was quite speechless with wonder and his little eyes stuck out on stalks. Then there came a sound from near the mainland: 'Hoo-oo-oooo-oo!'

'Oh dear,' said Melody, 'that's the boat come to take us home.'

'Silly old boat,' said Nelson, 'I want to stay.'

'The boat, she is for tomorrow,' said Otto. 'To-night is-a for the party. Let us enjoy. We go back to the Blue Cave, no?'

So they did, and the dancing went on long after bed-time till, as the old saying goes, 'the gunpowder ran out of the heels of their shoes'.

More Beaver Books

We hope you have enjoyed this Beaver Book. Here are some of the other titles:

Wilberforce the Whale Leslie Coleman's story about a young and jolly whale, Wilberforce, who sets off with his two young friends Melody the shrimp and Nelson the crab, on a visit to his Aunty Barnacle in Scotland. An amusing story for younger readers with illustrations by John Laing

Emil in the Soup Tureen Emil is always up to mischief of some sort, and the day he gets his head stuck in the soup tureen is just one of his really bad days. Astrid Lindgren's funny story for younger readers is illustrated by Bjorn Berg

Mr Bubbus and the Apple-green Engine Forester, the apple-green engine, was Mr Bubbus's pride and joy, but Sir Benjamin Bathbun was interested in steam engines too. . . . Joan Drake's amusing story for younger children is illustrated by Val Biro with his usual wit and humour

This is Ridiculous A Beaver original by Donald Bisset. Absurd and amusing stories for the youngest readers or for reading aloud; with illustrations by the author

Rhyme Time A Beaver original. Over 200 poems specially chosen by Barbara Ireson to introduce younger readers to the pleasures of reading verse. This lively collection is illustrated throughout by Lesley Smith

The Holiday Story Book A collection of funny and fantastic stories and limericks written and illustrated by Charlotte Hough for younger children

New Beavers are published every month and if you would like the *Beaver Bulletin* – which gives all the details – please send a stamped addressed envelope to:

Beaver Bulletin
The Hamlyn Group
Astronaut House
Feltham
Middlesex TW14 9AR